Martin Stanev

THE PLANET IN A PICKLE JAR

Flying Eye Books

Our Grandma lived a lonely and quiet life.

She saved up all her words and smiles
for when we came to visit.

She cooked boring meals.

And told the longest stories.

Her house was as dull and ordinary as she was.

All she did was shop,

knit,

and make jars of pickles.

She never did anything fun.

One evening, Grandma wanted to tell us something important, so we tried to look interested.

Children, our world is very fragile. If we don't do anything to preserve it, it will slowly fade away...

until all that is left is concrete, smoke and dust.

For once, we listened.

That night, we gazed at the world outside,
thinking about Grandma's words.

Suddenly, a star fell from the sky and vanished.

Were things already
starting to fade away?

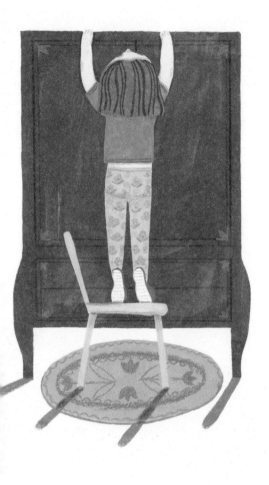

We rushed to ask Grandma,
only to find she'd vanished too.

Grandma?

We searched high and low, but all we could find was . . .

AARRHHH!

Searching for a place to hide,
we discovered a mysterious door leading
down some stairs we'd never seen before.

We hurried inside, hoping they would lead us to Grandma.

Suddenly, we heard
something at the end
of the corridor.

After what felt like a lifetime,
we emerged into the most incredible room.
It was a huge sanctuary. Had our Grandma
built this? Maybe she wasn't so boring after all . . .

We squeezed her close, glad that she hadn't vanished like the star and everything else in her story.

So that's what we did.

We began helping our Grandma to preserve the wonders of our planet, one pickle jar at a time.

About the Author

Inspired by vintage illustrated books, history, the natural world and childhood nostalgia, Martin Stanev creates playful and emotion-rich characters that inhabit immersive and magical worlds. Originally from Bulgaria, he moved to the UK where he graduated with a degree in illustration from Falmouth University. Martin now lives just south of the Lake District, UK, where the landscape brings back memories of home.

If you like this, you'll love...

978-1-83874-136-5

978-1-83874-105-1

978-1-912497-42-3